A separation anxiety s

Jasper Lizard wants to Stay Home

Written by **Ashley Bartley**   Illustrated by **Brian Martin**

Jasper Lizard Wants to Stay Home
Text and Illustrations Copyright © 2023 by Father Flanagan's Boys' Home
ISBN: 978-0-938510-95-6

Published by the Boys Town Press
13603 Flanagan Blvd., Boys Town, NE 68010

Author photo credit: Kathy Denton Photography

For a Boys Town Press catalog, call **1-800-282-6657**
or visit our website: **BoysTownPress.org**

Publisher's Cataloging-in-Publication Data

Names: Bartley, Ashley, author. | Martin, Brian (Brian Michael), 1978- illustrator.

Title: Jasper Lizard wants to stay home : a separation anxiety story / written by Ashley Bartley ; illustrated by Brian Martin.

Identifiers: ISBN: 978-0-938510-95-6

Subjects: LCSH: Lizards–Juvenile fiction. | School attendance–Juvenile fiction. | Separation anxiety in children–Juvenile fiction. | Fear in children–Juvenile fiction. | Stress management for children–Juvenile fiction. | School children–Juvenile fiction. | Anxiety in children–Juvenile fiction. | Counseling in elementary education–Juvenile fiction. | Success in children–Juvenile fiction. | Children–Life skills guides–Juvenile fiction. | CYAC: Lizards–Fiction. | Schools–Fiction. | Separation anxiety–Fiction. | Fear–Fiction. | Stress management-Fiction. | Anxiety –Fiction. | Success–Fiction. | Conduct of life–Fiction. | LCGFT: Children's stories. | BISAC: JUVENILE FICTION / Social Themes / Emotions & Feelings. | JUVENILE FICTION / Social Themes / New Experience. | JUVENILE FICTION / Social Themes / Self-Esteem & Self-Reliance. | JUVENILE FICTION / School & Education.

Classification: LCC: PZ7.1.B37289 J37 2023 | DDC: [E]–dc23

Printed in the United States
10 9 8 7 6 5 4 3 2 1

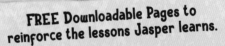

FREE Downloadable Pages to reinforce the lessons Jasper learns.

ACCESS:
https://www.boystownpress.org/book-downloads

ENTER:
Your first and last names
Email address
Code: 938510jlwtsh956
Check "yes" to receive emails to ensure your email link is received.

Boys Town Press is the publishing division of Boys Town, a national organization serving children and families.

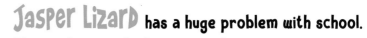
Jasper Lizard has a huge problem with school.
For weeks now, he has refused to go.
He stays home playing video games
or binge-watching his favorite reptile show.

"You're missing way too much school," his dad yells.
"And you're making yourself sick with your sobs.
These morning tantrums are exhausting you
and causing us to be late for our jobs!"

"I don't want to go to school ever again!
It's too much work, so I quit!
There are tests all the time, and the work never ends.
I'm not smart enough to do it."

Jasper scampers away and hides in his room,
using camouflage to blend in with his bed.
"Maybe if Dad can't find me, I won't have to go.
I can stay here and play games instead."

"Jasper, I know you're in there!
You're hiding because you feel scared.
Staying home isn't going to solve your problems
just because you feel unprepared."

6

"You're falling behind on your work.
There's a good chance you won't even pass.
You can't possibly keep up your grades
when you miss so much time from class!

"It's hard to make or keep friends
if you don't see them every day.
You'll feel more connected once you learn all their names,
and the fun games they like to play."

"I'd rather stay home," Jasper whines.
"I'm not ready to go back, not just yet.
There's so much work I must make up,
and a million school rules that I know I'll forget.

"I don't want to go back! I want to stay home!
Plus, I don't have my homework done today.
I promise, tomorrow, I'll go back to school.
Please, let me just stay home and play!"

"Okay, but remember, you promised.
Come morning, you must be ready to go.
We'll spend this one last day at home,
and then it's off to school tomorrow."

In the morning, Jasper wakes up moaning,
"I feel sick, and I need to stay home!
You can leave me here while you go to work.
I'll be fine being home on my own."

"Don't be silly, Jasper. You promised you'd go.
Your attendance is already low.
Walking in late is a bad habit, too.
Grab your backpack, it's time to go."

When Dad pulls up to school,
Jasper freezes and refuses to get out.

"Jasper, you're holding up the car line.
I don't understand what this tantrum's about."

"Is there a bully at school? Is the classwork too hard?
Haven't you always liked school before?
Are you having problems on the bus?
Is school too easy? Or do you just find it a bore?"

"It's not a bully," Jasper sniffs and sobs.
"Leaving you makes me lonely and sad.
 My head aches. My belly hurts, and my stomach's in knots.
 But it'll go away if you take me back to our pad."

"Don't make me stay! I don't want to go.
I want to be at home – with you!
I'm dizzy. My skin looks pale.
I think it must be the flu!"

"Okay," Dad sighs. "Since you're not feeling well,
we'll go home and just take it easy.
No tablet, no games, only your makeup work,
and some crackers if you're still feeling queasy."

That evening, Jasper dresses for football.
He tells everyone he feels fine.
"Oh no, we can't let you go. You're still sick!
You'll have to miss practice this time."

17

"But Coach said if I'm not at practice,
I won't play in Saturday's BIG game!
I promise I'm feeling better already.
Without me, my team's not the same!"

18

On game day, Jasper blends in with the bench
as his team tries their best on the field.
He feels guilty because he pretended to be sick.
Embarrassed, he tries staying concealed.

A teammate spots him after the game.

"Well, we lost our winning streak.
Hey, aren't you supposed to be on my bus?
I haven't seen you riding it all this week."

"Sit with me Monday! I'll bring my new toy.
Our bus driver has a new rule.
As long as we put them back in our backpacks,
we can play with toys on our way to school!"

Looking forward to having a new friend,
Jasper packs his favorite toy for the bus.
Mom and Dad are proud he got ready
without making his usual fuss.

Jasper waits with his dad for the bus to arrive,
but his worries make him want to cry.
When the bus pulls up, the driver smiles,
and Jasper and his dad say a quick goodbye.

Having a toy from home in his backpack
helps Jasper get through the day.
But his teacher, Ms. Crow, sets one condition:
"You mustn't take it out to play."

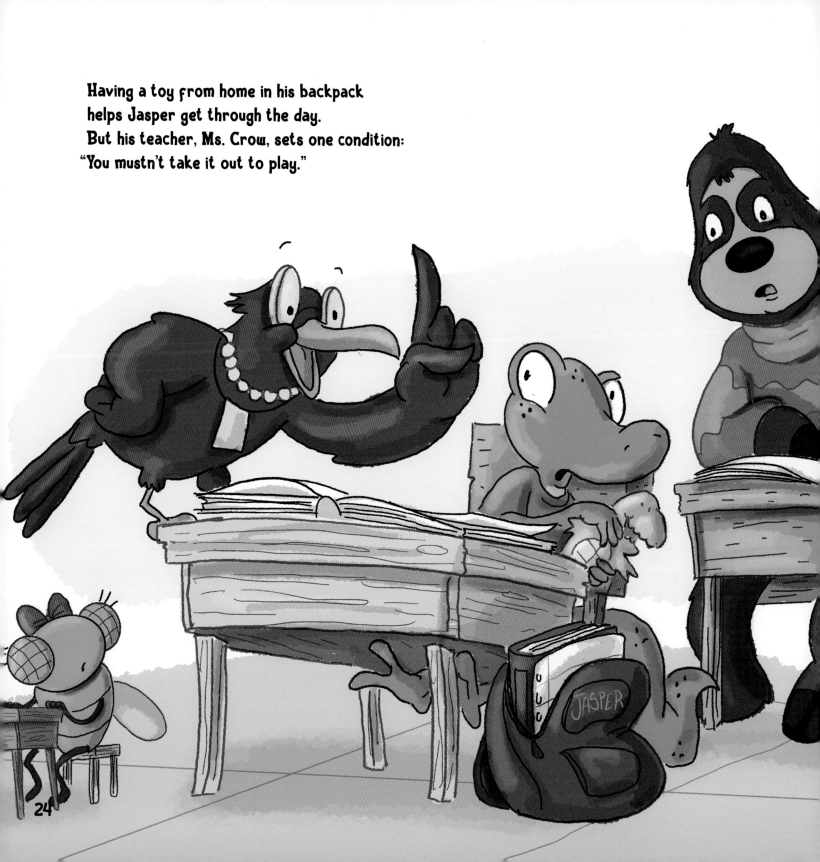

Ms. Crow then gets another idea: Jasper can help Opal.
Jasper can take a job off her very full work plate.

"Would you be our new office messenger?
It's a morning job, so you must never be late."

"I'll do it!" Jasper answers proudly,
puffing out his colorful throat.
"Great! Walk to the office with Remi.
He'll show you where to take this class note."

Jasper stays busy the rest of the morning,
catching up on the work he has missed.
"I'll focus on one assignment at a time
until I get through my whole list."

His new friends make him feel welcome.
Sugar Hummingbird takes him under her wing.
"I'll introduce you to all of the kids
and swoop in to help if you need anything!"

Jasper enjoys recess, specials, and lunch.
He feels awesome about having a fresh start.
With an eye for design and a strong sense of color,
of course, his favorite new class is ART!

It's okay to be sad and miss home during class,
especially after long breaks or weekends.
It helps having something from home, or a routine,
or looking forward to seeing good friends.

Now Jasper gets on the bus every day,
after a hug goodbye from Mom and Dad.
He sits with his friend and looks forward to class
thinking, "This school thing is really not so bad."

TIPS FOR PARENTS & EDUCATORS

Many elementary students struggle with separation anxiety, school anxiety, or school refusal. This can negatively impact their attendance as well as the cohesion and sense of community in the classroom. Working together, parents, caregivers, and educators can support and help children have more successful transitions to school each day. Using these strategies can make a difference.

1 **Arrange a school or classroom tour and/or a visit with the teacher.** Orientation activities, especially at the start of a new school year, can be opportunities to familiarize kids with their school environment and calm their worries.

2 **Use the school bus or have someone else do the school drop-off, if possible.** Kids often handle separation and goodbyes better at home than at the school door.

3 **Have a meaningful goodbye ritual.** Consider using a loving phrase to signal the transition. Don't linger or sneak away. Instead, make a quick exit after saying goodbye.

4 **Stick to a consistent routine before school.** Routines and boundaries can be comforting to children because they eliminate questions about expectations or the "what-ifs."

5 **Speak positively about the school and teachers.** Keep the focus on the upcoming school day.

6 **Encourage children to make connections at school.** This will help them feel like they are part of a community. Assigning special morning jobs also can foster a sense of ownership and responsibility.

7 **Use a transition/comfort object.** A special object that can be worn or kept in a backpack, such as a necklace, photograph, or stuffed animal, can be soothing and comforting. Just remember that the object might get lost or damaged, so choose the object accordingly. Check in with other parents and teachers for suggestions on what is/isn't helpful.

8 **Identify the root of the problem.** Talk about what's bothering the child or if there is a specific concern, such as bullying. When physical symptoms of anxiety persist, consult a medical provider to determine if there is a valid medical concern.

BOYS TOWN®
Saving Children Healing Families

For more parenting information, visit boystown.org/parenting.

Boys Town Press books
Kid-friendly books for teaching social skills

978-1-944882-87-7

978-1-944882-57-0

978-1-944882-73-0

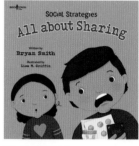

978-1-944882-96-9

A book series by Ashley Bartley for grades PreK-5 that teaches
children self-care, self-control, and self-determination.

A book series to help kids master social situations.

Downloadable Activities
Go to BoysTownPress.org to download.

978-1-944882-92-1

978-1-9-44882-42-6

978-1-944882-54-9

978-1-944882-69-3

OTHER TITLES:
Freddie the Fly: Motormouth
Freddie the Fly: Connecting
the Dots
Freddie the Fly: Bee On,
Buzz Off

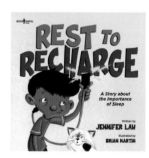

978-1-944882-91-4

For information on Boys Town and its Education Model,
Common Sense Parenting®, and training programs:
boystowntraining.org | boystown.org/parenting
training@BoysTown.org | 1-800-545-5771

For parenting and educational
books and other resources:
BoysTownPress.org
btpress@BoysTown.org | 1-800-282-6657